PERFECTLY MARTHA

Susan Meddaugh

Houghton Mifflin Company Boston 2004

Walter Lorraine Books

For Marguerite
and
for Vicki,
the voice of Martha

Walter Lorraine Books

www.houghtonmifflinbooks.com

Library of Congress Cataloging-in-Publication Data
Meddaugh, Susan.
  Perfectly Martha / Susan Meddaugh.
    p. cm.
"Walter Lorraine Books"—Verso t.p.
  Summary: Martha discovers how the Perfect Pup Institute turns dogs into
obedient robots and then does something about it.
  ISBN 0-618-37857-X
  [1. Dogs—Fiction. 2. Dogs—Training—Fiction.] I. Title.
PZ7.M51273Pe 2004
[E]—dc22
                                                        2003015161

Printed in the United States of America
WOZ 10 9 8 7 6 5 4 3 2 1

"What did you say?" asked Mother.

"I mean, soup, please," said Martha.
Mother smiled and fixed breakfast for Martha and Skits.
The two dogs began every day with tasty bowls of alphabet soup.
As usual, the soup went straight to Skits's stomach.

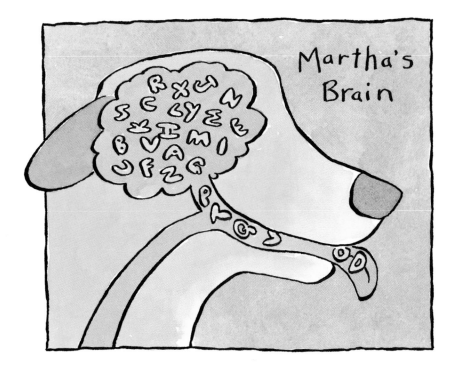

But the letters in Martha's soup went to her brain.
And Martha spoke.

After breakfast, Martha and Skits strolled downtown.
On Main Street they joined a crowd of people.
"Friends," said a man in a green suit, "what do dogs want?"
Before Martha could answer, the man continued.
"They want to scatter trash on pickup day, sleep on the furniture, and drink from the toilet. They drool and bark and scratch their fleas. And they would always rather chase a squirrel than come when you call."

Then the man said:
"Is that what people want?
Your dog may be your best friend,
but he could be better. I, Otis
Weaselgraft, will show you how.
Sir Lancelot," he called. "Come."
A sturdy pug approached the dog
trainer.

"Sit!" said Otis Weaselgraft.

"Get down!" he said.

"Roll over!"

"Beg!"

"Hop on one paw!"

After this impressive demonstration, Otis Weaselgraft said:
"Sign up today for my THREE-STEP TRAINING PROGRAM.
Tomorrow you'll have a *perfect pup,* just like Sir Lancelot."

"Hmmmph!" Martha said to Skits.

Word of the new dog trainer and his amazing program traveled from neighbor to neighbor. Soon half the dogs in town were enrolled at the Perfect Pup Institute.

At the Perfect Pup Institute, Martha and Skits slipped in to observe the latest graduating class. They watched as every dog obeyed every command.

They sat.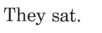

They got down.

They rolled over.

They begged.

They hopped on one paw.

Finally Otis Weaselgraft placed a dog biscuit in front of each graduate.
"Wait," he said, and every dog waited.

Skits couldn't believe his eyes.
With a hungry "Woof!" he bounded forward and gobbled up every single biscuit.

Otis Weaselgraft was not upset. It was a perfect opportunity to show off his program. He placed another biscuit in front of each dog.
"Good dogs may now eat their biscuits," he said. "Chew slowly. And, please, no crumbs and no drool."
Four perfect dogs did exactly as they were told.

Outside, Martha consulted with Skits.

Martha didn't see Otis Weaselgraft's quiet partner, Dr. Pablum. "A talking dog!" he gasped. "I've got to find out how she does that."

The next morning Martha began an investigation of the
Perfect Pup Institute. She was wondering how to get inside
when Dr. Pablum swung open the door.
"Come right in!" he said to Martha.

Dr. Pablum escorted Martha to his laboratory. But before she had
a chance to look around, he pushed her into a crate and locked it.
"Speak!" said Dr. Pablum. "I know you can."
Martha did not hesitate.

"I knew it!" said Dr. Pablum. "Weaselgraft!" he shouted.
"A talking dog! I'll be famous!"

Otis Weaselgraft came into the lab. He looked at Martha.

"You're working too hard," Otis Weaselgraft growled at Dr. Pablum.
"Get rid of this mutt. She's not even a paying customer."
But Dr. Pablum had big plans for Martha.

Otis Weaselgraft stomped out of the room. He soon returned with a dog who looked like Sir Lancelot. But this dog wasn't acting like Sir Lancelot.

"Fix him!" Otis Weaselgraft snapped at Dr. Pablum. "We can't have this happening during a demonstration."

Dr. Pablum put Sir Lancelot into a crate next to Martha and left with the pug's collar.

"Sir Lancelot," said Martha.

"Burt," said the pug, in Dog. "They call me Sir Lancelot, but my real name is Burt."

He slumped in his cage.

"I used to run with the big dogs," he said mournfully. "But look at me now. A demo-dog. No better than a robot."

Before Burt could answer, Dr. Pablum returned with his collar. He slipped it onto the struggling pug.

When Dr. Pablum left again, Martha called to Burt.

But this time Burt didn't respond. He just looked straight ahead.

It's the collar! thought Martha.
She watched as Otis Weaselgraft and Dr. Pablum embarked
on their Three-Step Perfect Pup Program.

Step one:
They removed the dogs' collars.

Step two:
They attached a tiny object to the inside of each collar.

Step three:
They put the collars back on.

Now every dog was staring straight ahead. No tails wagged, and no fleas were scratched.

"Come," said Dr. Pablum, and all the dogs followed him to the front room.

Otis Weaselgraft opened the crate and pushed Martha out the back door of the Perfect Pup Institute.

When Dr. Pablum returned to his lab he was horrified to discover the empty crate.

Where is my talking dog!?!

"Really, Pablum," said Otis Weaselgraft. "There's no such thing as a talking dog."
Dr. Pablum was *furious*.

He raced to the back door to look for Martha.

"I'll tell you MY One-Step Talking Dog Secret," Martha said,
"if you do one thing for me."
She whispered in his ear.

"Yes," said Dr. Pablum, who was still very angry,
"I'll do it."

In the front room the owners had gathered to see their
pets perform.

"Otis," Dr. Pablum said, "your collar is a little crooked."
He reached up and made a small adjustment.

"There," he said, giving the back of the collar a pat. "Now
you're perfect."

Then, from someone hidden in
the shadows, came a command.

Four dogs sat. And so did Otis Weaselgraft.

"Get down!" said the voice.

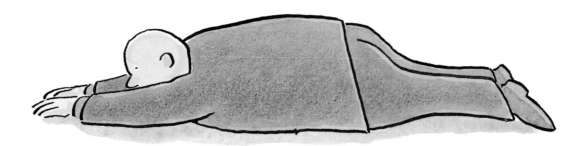

"Roll over!" she said.

"Beg!"

"Hop on one paw . . .
I mean foot!"

Finally Martha said, "Speak. Tell the truth about the Perfect Pup Program."
Otis Weaselgraft began to talk.

I'm not really a dog trainer. We put a microchip in your dog's collar. The ROBOROVER Brain Blocker. Shuts off every part of the brain except the OBEDIENCE lobe. Turns dogs into furry robots. Lasts about a month... just long enough to take your money and move to the next state. Tried it on cats last year. The Purrfect Pussy Cat Program. What a CATastrophe! Cats don't even have obedience lobes.

ARF

ARF

ARF

While the angry owners were removing the collars
from their pets, Dr. Pablum cornered Martha.
"Quick," he said, "what's the secret?"
And Martha, who never broke a promise, told him.

"Very funny," said Dr. Pablum. "Now tell me the real secret."
But, seeing the owners approaching, he beat a hasty retreat.
Dr. Pablum was still puzzling over what Martha meant by
"soup" as he boarded a bus out of town.

Things are back to normal in Martha's neighborhood. Most of the Double PPs had to admit that having a perfect pup was really no fun. Something very important was missing. So once again dogs scatter the trash and drink from the toilet. They bark and scratch their fleas and sleep on the furniture.

But they also greet their owners with wagging tails and slobbery kisses.

Isn't that what people really want?

WOOF!

ARF!